Inspiration

To dear Joan,
Remembering with gratitude
how you both helped me
all those years ago.........
Love, Anne Beer

Inspiration
by
Anne Beer

Blue Poppy Publishing 2020

I defy you not to laugh
when you reach page 2 !!

Transcribed by various kind volunteers
Edited by Sarah Dawes
Cover photograph – Anne Beer
Illustrations – Anne Beer
Cover design – Oliver Tooley
Typesetting – Oliver Tooley

All contributors donated their time and skills

FIRST EDITION

ISBN: 978-1-911438-69-4 Paperback

ISBN: 978-1-911438-59-5 Hardcover

Contents

Introduction

By Oliver Tooley

I first had the pleasure of meeting Anne after starting up a writers' group in my hometown of Ilfracombe. I think it is worth going back a little further to explain that, while there were several writing groups which met (as they still do) in Barnstaple library, no such group existed in Ilfracombe. Being aware that there are many residents of 'Combe who do not drive, I thought it worthwhile to provide a similar group for local residents who could not easily get to the larger town. One of the first members of this group was Anne Beer.

Anne quickly established herself as a veritable doyenne of beautiful creative writing on practically any subject. As a group, I hope I can speak for everyone when I say that we look forward to hearing her writing every month. She can make us cry at will and make us laugh with equal ease. A great deal of what she writes is taken from real life, with many a personal recollection of her own long and eventful journey on Planet Earth.

We have implored her to write her entire biography, but we may have to content ourselves with gleaning what we can from the little two- or three-page snapshots that we get every now and then. If we do ever get the full story it has the potential to make compelling reading and perhaps a future bestseller.

Anne herself is a demure and self-effacing, sprightly lady who defies her advancing years. She is quite computer illiterate and does not even possess a typewriter, at the time of writing this, let alone a PC or laptop. Anne is kind, quiet, and devoted to her assistance dog, Ellie, who helps to keep her calm in difficult social situations. Most notable of her many endearing characteristics is her complete failure to realise just how wonderful she really is. This modesty sometimes manifests itself as self-loathing and, for this reason, I beg you dear reader, if you enjoy this book, to write a review.

BUT…

I am going to ask an awful lot of you.

I would dearly love you to write a handwritten letter to Anne, so that she can enjoy the tactile and visceral pleasure of holding your words in her hand and reading them from the page.

I know this is a lot to ask, but I suspect that many of you will make the special effort once you have read Anne's stories, particularly those true stories relating to her own life.

You may address a letter to Blue Poppy Publishing; the address can be found at the back of the book.

P.S. While reading this book, you will probably need to keep a box of tissues to hand, just in case.

Kings & Queens Festival Madness

South Molton Creative Writing Group
August 2014

The country vicar strode into the village hall, his benign fixed look pinned on his face. He would much rather be in the overgrown vicarage garden where no one could find him.

Nothing much happened in this quiet backwater and now he had been summoned to a parish meeting to nod his head in acceptance to a suggested festival to celebrate the Queen's coronation.

He knew in advance that the gathering would be made up mostly of elderly ladies, still wearing pre-war frocks and lengthy bloomers. This latter observation proved fruitful as, upon entering the hall, Miss Higginbottom who had (thank God, thought the vicar) moved away some time ago, had returned for this meeting and, sitting with legs splayed out and vast acres of pink bloomerage on display shouted out, "Remember me, Vicar?"

REMEMBER ME
VICAR?

The vicar felt a blush rising up from his clerical collar and Miss Higginbottom took this to mean that the vicar had a crush on her!

After carefully negotiating the wooden knots that stood up in the ancient floorboards, the vicar took his seat and listened to the suggestions put forward for the festival.

The felt hats and handbag brigade wobbled their chins, creaked their corsets, and drank stewed tea from thick china mismatching cups, and ate stale biscuits from the same tin that had been opened and shut numerous times, making for soft cardboard dunkers.

Belinda the bunting lady would do her usual decorations in red, white, and blue; the cake stall and white elephant was swiftly dealt with, and the centrepiece of the festival was to be the royal tableau conveyed on Farmer Giles' tractor and trailer on to the village green. The schoolchildren would sing *Land of Hope and Glory* as the whole display arrived, and the procession would duly take pride of place in the food-laden marquee.

"Ah," said the vicar, "very good, but who will be on the royal tableau? We need a queen, ladies-in-waiting…"

"And a king," said someone.

"No, no, there's no king," said the vicar. "Some page boys perhaps."

"But you can't leave Prince Philip out!" gushed Mrs Tweedy.

"Yes you can. No one will know. After all, it is the Queen's special day." And so it went on.

3

The meeting broke up to be reconvened in a week, by which time a queen would be found and a Britannia as well.

Everyone wanted to be the Queen, no matter their shape, size, or age. Squabbles broke out, a decision could not be made so the vicar said that the best way was to put the name of everyone who wished to be queen into a hat, and this was to take place at the reconvened meeting.

The following week, an excited but tense atmosphere greeted the vicar as he entered the crowded village hall. Some of the ladies had had their hair permed since last week, pretending they hadn't of course. Even Mrs Clumpy had exchanged her lisle stockings for a pair of nylons. Some wore lipstick gone wonky and several costumes emerged, smelling of mothballs.

Miss Higginbottom had at least changed her bloomers since last week as she was now perched on an infant's chair spread-eagled in a blue pair of drawers.

All the unbroken adult chairs were occupied, as this was such a popular meeting, so the last to arrive either stood, or sat on collapsible card tables, or infant seats.

After the erratic tea urn had uttered a sigh and a near explosion, the excited ladies drank their tea, smudged their lipstick, primped their hair, and nursed their handbags to their bosoms in nervous anticipation.

Clearing his throat and running his finger round inside his clerical collar, the vicar shook up the hat containing all the names.

"First we will draw for who will represent Britannia."

A hush fell over the eager faces. The vicar's long, bony, white fingers drew out a name.

"Mrs Clumpy is to be Britannia," he announced.

A smug look came over Mrs Clumpy's face as she looked around.

"Now for the Queen." The vicar silently prayed as his hand went into the hat that it would at least be someone sensible and a tiny bit good looking.

"Miss Higginbottom!"

Everyone gasped, then laughed and looked around to Miss Higginbottom who really did think that the vicar had a crush on her after all and had 'arranged it'. She was hot and flustered and blushing; felt triumphant as she gloated around at the assembled women. The vicar was blushing too, with embarrassment, but Miss Higginbottom took this to mean that he was actually in love with her.

She floated home on air, despite her heavy lace-up shoes, and hitched her bloomers up under her armpits before they slipped below her knees.

A frenzied month of activity followed to prepare for the festival. Costumes were made amidst disastrous fittings. The jellies, blancmanges, the cucumber and fish-paste sandwiches, and more, were at last delicately piled up in the marquee. The time had come for the grand opening of the festival.

Unfortunately, due to the inclemency of the weather, this took place inside the marquee where a steady drip from a leak in the roof put the squawky microphone out of action.

The bunting hung forlornly outside whilst mud squelched inside.

Shouting, the vicar hoped that everyone would enjoy themselves and as soon as there was a break in the weather the main attraction, the royal tableau, would arrive.

Meanwhile, to pass the time, a couple of young schoolboys decided it would be great fun to saw away at the guy ropes supporting the marquee, and to this end lay prone in their short grey trousers, caps pulled down, covered in mud, pocket knives working furiously. The object being to attain at least partial marquee collapse, wriggle under the canvas, and scoff the grub during the ensuing chaos.

Outside, Major Fartloose, retired, announced that the royal tableau was approaching by giving a wavery half-strangled blow on his bugle. Everyone jostled to get outside the marquee to witness this event as the rain had stopped.

'Phut-phut-phut... phut-phut-phut...' Farmer Giles was in his most important element, his Fordson tractor pulling the trailer on which the tableau was arranged.

His old flat cap was such a permanent feature that no one knew if he had any hair or not. With a self-satisfied grin, he bounced around on the tractor's seat, about to make his grand entry.

In the slippery conditions, a massive pothole caught him unawares and caused the lynch pin to jump out, parting tractor from trailer, but being so wrapped up in his glory moment, he was unaware as his old Fordson chugged along towards the awaiting crowd outside the marquee. The shouts from the people left stranded on the trailer behind him went unnoticed as the noise of the tractor drowned them out. Besides which, Farmer Giles thought that his Fordson was pulling really easily now, better even than rehearsals! Oh, this was a feather in his cap indeed!

But what was that silly Major Whatshisname, retired, doing blethering about and waving that 'past it' bugle thing for?

"Gor darn it," muttered Farmer Giles, "I'll run 'ee down, give over."

"Look behind you, man!" shouted the major.

Farmer Giles came to a shuddering halt.

"And turn off that blasted machine!"

Farmer Giles scratched his head, nearly revealing what was or was not under his cap, and faced the crowd gathered outside the marquee. They were laughing fit to burst and pointing to the stranded trailer.

The vicar streaked across the sodden grass towards the trailer. The tableau was in complete disarray as Britannia, alias Mrs Clumpy, had got her trident stuck up the Queen's gusset. Miss 'Queen' Higginbottom was spread out on the floor of the trailer clasping her papier maché orb and sceptre, with her crown drooping over one eye and her gown up around her middle. The page boys shrieked with laughter; the little maids with their pretty dresses were wailing because they were covered in mud. A reluctant Prince Philip, borrowed from the senior boys' school, couldn't help for laughing and finally collapsed in a hopeless heap.

The vicar, whose clerical collar had popped out with all his athletic effort, came to Miss 'Queen' Higginbottom's aid. He tactfully pulled her dress over her bloomers, which he tried not to notice were a greyer shade of white.

"Oh vicar! How kind! What a gentleman you are to help me!" exclaimed Miss Higginbottom, who blushed so hotly she looked as if she were about to go into labour.

The vicar put his arms around her and lifted her up. He felt really sorry for her and stumbled with her towards the crowd, who all thought it was part of the show, a deliberate parting tractor from trailer and the rescuing of the Queen by the vicar. Everyone was laughing, clapping, or rolled up clutching their sides. The vicar by now was very red, and Miss Higginbottom was planning a spring wedding in her mind. Nothing could have been further from the vicar's, however, as he unceremoniously dropped his heavy load on that damned major's foot.

More laughter ensued and, very gradually, the backdrop of the marquee began doing a slow collapse as people proceeded to enter and enjoy the spread of food and a huge celebration cake.

"The vicar will now say grace," the major declared.

The re-adjusted vicar bowed his head and said, "For what we are about to receive…" when the whole marquee slithered down one side, squashing jellies, and wobbling blancmanges. Plates of sandwiches had disappeared, and the celebration cake had vanished. Sudden panic ensued as people rushed outside. The local baker who had made the beautiful cake feared he had now missed his moment of recognition. The children's choir couldn't continue singing '*Land of Hope and Glory*' for laughing at grown-ups in posh clothes trying to run sedately in the mud away from the marquee.

"Oh my cake, my beautiful cake!" bemoaned the baker.

"And all our hard work with the sandwiches," fretted the tea ladies.

"What are we to do?"

"Oh look!" said one lady, pointing at two very muddy boys carrying a tablecloth between them.

"That's my cloth from one of the trestle tables!"

On closer inspection, inside the cloth, there was the celebration cake in all its glory, almost completely unharmed, plus plates of sandwiches.

"Unbelievable!" said the vicar. "What quick thinking by you boys to rescue all this food on such an important occasion! Well done, you've saved the day!"

Five Silences

South Molton Creative Writing Group
June 2015

1   Silence is golden. There's so much that I could reveal and say about this person. I know too much about their scheming ways, the lies, the deceit, their polished performance at being so charming, buying rounds in the pub and wasting money and leaving me penniless. I should know, he was my ex-husband. The list is endless; but how can I ruin his new wife-to-be's happiness? She looks to be so much in love, she doesn't know who I am. Oh the temptation to tell her as she looks at her flashing diamond ring! He stole my jewellery and sold it in a second-hand shop in Bideford years ago; perhaps he's bought that ring with the proceeds? I don't think so: money ran through his fingers like water.

"We're having the reception in the pub," she informs us. "It's 'The Ship on Launch' in Bideford."

Everyone in our ladies' club is invited for the evening bash. It will be more like 'The Ship Aground' by the time they're finished!

Silence is golden. The temptation to reveal all is too much. I leave the ladies' club never to return.

2   It's a white-out. The moor is muffled in a big snow blanket. The white of it shines ghostly in the moonlight as if lit through a veil.

The black sky is pinpricked by millions of glittering stars.

No wind, no movement, nothing stirs, not even an owl. The sound of silence is all around.

3   So many lives in the Resistance movement depended on the prisoner remaining silent. So much torture he endured for their sakes.

His screams could be heard beyond the prison walls, but he'd got what it takes as his screams became sobs, his sobs crumbled, and he died, his lips sealed for eternity.

4   "Silence in court!" the judge's double chins wobbled as he brought the gavel down with an irritated bang.

Days of summing up had come to an end. The sentence was about to be announced.

A pregnant silence fell upon the hushed room.

5   I've taken a vow of silence
I wished I never had
'Cos life within these convent walls
Is driving me quite mad!

Harvest Home

South Molton Creative Writing Group
October 2014
Write a piece including the words: Strict
Order, Fire Exit, Curtain, Autumn, Mantlepiece,
Serendipity.

The golden autumn sun pierced through the early morning mist, its warm breath clinging to the narrow cobbled alleyway of ancient cottages. Colourful fuchsias and geraniums spilled out of window boxes catching the last of October's warmth.

Muted voices drifted out of open windows and the whole place basked in the late mellow yellow, apart from the shadows beneath the walls where the sun would not reach again until next spring.

It was amongst these shadows that a family passed, almost unnoticed, having been evicted by Strict Order from the local council. They had lived in Serendipity Cottage at the end of the cobbled alleyway for generations.

The sweet old cottage was being gutted, and as the family departed, they paid a fond farewell to the ancient mantlepiece now incongruously dumped in the tiny rear garden. Their cosy home of warm floorboards and velvet curtains, a damped down fireplace on a winter's night, was gone, and just the shell remained.

With no money, and no belongings, they carried on down towards the quay. No one welcomed them and they were hard pressed to find somewhere safe for the night. They thought about jumping on a fishing boat, but the tide was out, and climbing the ropes in broad daylight was risky, but even worse at night when it would be high water.

The people at the Seamen's Mission were friendly though, and sometimes left cakes and biscuits out after a coffee morning, but the mission was closed for re-decorating.

As they passed the church they heard the organist practising harvest hymns. Creeping inside, they slipped into a pew and kept quiet.

The church was decorated for the Harvest Festival. There was food! The unmistakable aroma of harvest things filled the building. The family hid themselves until the playing had stopped and it wasn't until late in the day before they came out of their hiding place to feast on something to eat. They just hoped that there wasn't too much tinned stuff as was the trend of late. 'PLEASE DONATE NON-PERISHABLES FOR THE HOMELESS' it said on the church notice board, and they hadn't a tin opener between them!

There was plenty of fruit, a few vegetables and a giant pumpkin which was no good at all, but upon the altar was a big, beautiful, harvest loaf – praise the Lord! They were so hungry and set to and ate this timely sent manna from heaven.

In the vestry they found water in the sink plus a dripping tap. Replete, they rested on a pile of musty cassocks. Here was a place they could return to if needed: a refuge, a bolthole.

But for now they would play it safe, or so they thought, and returned to the outside world by squeezing under the Fire Exit door, narrowly avoiding death from the waiting neighbourhood cat.

The Picture

Creative Writing Carers' Group
We were given a picture and asked to describe the
life of the woman in it.

When Megan married her childhood sweetheart at 16, the future looked rosy, stretching out for ever into endless summer in their kingdom of heaven thatched cottage that sat comfortably into the landscape. Now she was alone, so alone in that landscape; carrying the heavy weight of the well bucket that might just as well be the weight around her heart. A widow now, at just 17, her darling Jack gone, in an instant, trampled by a bull.

She scorned widow's weeds but hid her fair hair under the cotton cottager's head dress, her lithe body hampered by the heavy wooden clogs. With ducks, hens, geese, and produce to see to, she laboured from dawn to dusk, blotting out her misery.

Inside the cottage she kicked off her clogs and cooled her feet on the flagstone floor of the kitchen whilst pondering her future. Sweat and tears mingled, coursing down her face; oh for an answer!

The geese announced the arrival of her friend. Megan jumped up to see Maisie approaching, full of excitement.

"Megan!" she cried, "Dry your tears, the fair is coming to Gooseberry Green. You mustn't weep forever. Besides, the fortune teller will be there again; and everything she told me last year came true! Why don't you see her as well?"

The colourful fair spilled around the green, the fragrance of trampled grass mingled with the smells of hog roasts, potatoes, sweetmeats, horses, and ale.

"Will ye be wanting the runes, cards, or crystal ball?" asked the grumpy fortune teller. "The crystal ball will reveal the most, but it also costs the most."

Megan was transfixed by the gypsy's eyes that now saw into her very soul. It was very close in the tent with all of its thick rich drapes that muffled the sounds outside. Inexplicably, Megan and the gypsy woman became as one mind, each seeing into the other.

"I'll give you the ball reading for nothing, as I feel you must know of this great revelation which I sense comin' your way soon. Place your hand firmly on the ball, for that way I can see your palm enlarged as well."

Although hot and sweaty, Megan found the crystal ball cool to the touch, sending a tingle up her arm. Transfixed, she saw the gypsy's eyes scrutinising her hand through the crystal ball.

"Before the swallows fly away, a pale stranger will ask you for water. Do not refuse. Give the water my dear and your life will be lifted above the mourning you now bear. You will become famous, but you will not know it. I see more, but best left unsaid for now."

Megan left the tent, her head swimming, glad of the fresh air, and rejoined her friend.

They strolled, arm in arm, homewards in the summer dusk, the night scented stock fragrant around the cottage, and the poultry already in their roosts. Megan only had to close their hut door and the two friends then shared their experiences by candlelight, about the fortune teller's revelations...

The season of mists and mellow fruitfulness was in full swing and the swallows lined up on the wall ready for departure to warmer climes when Megan, struggling with the well bucket, saw a man approaching out of the mist. It was the 'pale stranger'; so pale as to not be used to country ways. He wore a large satchel and bade Megan a good day. Putting down the heavy bucket, she eased her aching back and returned the greeting. He asked her for some water. Recalling the gypsy's prophecy she was entranced and, without hesitation, welcomed him into her kitchen. He was as pale as the lilies in the garden, his hair the colour of straw, completely the opposite of how her Jack had been, dark sunburnt skin and black hair.

'Give the water my dear and your life will be lifted...' the gypsy's words came back. She dipped the cup into the bucket and saw her own reflection in the water in the cup. He drank her reflection, and as he drank he swallowed her image. She was in him. It was done and nothing could undo it.

He was an artist from the city recovering from an accident and he made a sketch of her in her rustic kitchen as a thank you for the water. She filled his paint bottle and bade him farewell.

The swallows left the following morning. The sun pierced the first frost creating a mist. Megan's heart leapt with joy as the pale stranger re-appeared. They shared a cooked breakfast and made love in the little bedroom under the thatch. He asked permission to sketch and paint her as she went about her daily chores.

She was oh so lovely, but he could never capture her exquisite face. She abandoned herself to him: he came to stay, becoming less pale. He was working hard on a painting which he kept from her until he finished it, by which time he had become darker and more tanned. The darker he got, the more distant he became. The magic was slipping away. The finished painting revealed no face, just Megan walking towards the cottage with the bucket and the poultry for company.

And then he was gone, taking the picture with him. The now not-so-pale stranger returned to the city and Megan resumed her existence hoping to see him again.

The winter solstice and Christmas passed. Megan felt unwell. Maisie said it was because she was with child. The kitchen swam before her eyes and still the stranger didn't come.

She sold the cottage and got a passage, emigrating to where no one would know of her shame, where she could pose as an expectant widow.

The artist won national acclaim for his painting entitled *The Gooseberry Maiden*. It was the centrepiece in a London gallery, and many wanted to know who she was. His conscience got to him but too late, he realised, as he discovered that she had gone, gone forever, the cottage sad under its dripping thatch. He sold the picture to a publishing house.

Far away, Megan gave birth to a beautiful girl who grew up asking about her father. When Megan died, the beautiful girl returned to her mother's country hoping to find the cottage which Megan had so lovingly described.

Sitting in a tearoom, the beautiful girl absentmindedly traced her fingers over the place mat on the table. The mat bore the image of a country cottage and a young woman with a bucket and poultry walking towards the cottage, no face visible.

It looked idyllic. The owner of the tearoom said that it came from a painting and that the artist still lived in London and that this was the last picture that he had ever painted as he had withdrawn from society with a broken heart.

The artist sat alone in his dusty attic, the sun accentuating the shabbiness and old canvases stacked around the walls. His brushes were now stiff with age and his paints were hard, unused since that dream-like summer of bliss and the winter of dreadful loss when he found that Megan had gone.

A knocking sound interrupted his thoughts and for once he decided to answer the door. Clambering down the rickety staircase he saw a female shape through the frosted glass. He was in no decent attire, so he shouted, "Yes, who is it?"

"You don't know me, but I am looking for the artist who painted *The Gooseberry Maiden.*"

Unbolting the door he saw the spitting image of Megan, that exquisite face which he could never capture was there before him. It could not be Megan; so many years had passed, and this was a young woman before him.

"Who are you? What is your name?"

"My name is Megan Hope. Megan after my mother, and Hope, that she would see my father again. But sadly that was not to be. She died."

A bolt shot through the artist's heart at this news. One of sorrow, but mixed with elation as well…

"Come in, come in," he said excitedly. "I have an unfinished job to be done. May I paint your portrait?"

After many sittings, father and daughter got to know each other properly and catch up on what had happened over the years. Megan Hope made his dusty old home into a place to be proud of and he began painting again.

They named it 'Hope Studio' and in the gallery, beside her portrait, there hung a still-life of a plate of gooseberries.

Valentine and Red

South Molton Creative Writing Group
February 2015
Include the words 'Valentine' and 'Red' in a
piece of writing

Ellie had it all: the high life, the yacht, the mansions with a gravel drive, the various cars that would be parked there announcing that another set of celebrities had arrived.

For ten years she had been married to her showbiz husband, Lanzio, at first ecstatically. Then, loneliness set in each time she waved him off from the little grass landing strip behind their home as he piloted his own private plane on the way to clinch some deal or other. As his absences grew longer, Ellie's longing for a baby formed into a desperate yearning. They had been a passionate couple, but nothing had materialised.

She had secretly visited a Harley Street specialist who announced that she was completely normal and to relax and

24

not worry about it. She didn't tell Lanzio for fear of making him feel inadequate.

Oh how she longed to be a normal wife; to go shopping, go on the bus, chat to housewives. She would have to hide behind big sunglasses so as not to be recognised!

Suddenly, she decided to do something outrageous! Her chauffeur thought she had lost her mind when she asked him to order a taxi, after all, there were three cars she could have chosen from to go on a journey.

The bemused taxi driver turned up after getting past the security gate, mentally racking up what size tip he might receive after this job.

Ellie was dropped off on the posh side of town but walked with purpose in her headscarf and dark glasses to the not so posh part.

Here she became an ordinary person, listening to people having everyday conversations and bumping into one another. She was being quite decadent, mingling in the market then coming before a shop window that had a gorgeous display of red dresses for Valentine's Day.

As she stood, thinking, and staring into space, a male voice remarked that red would really suit her. She turned around and was stunned by the most handsome looking man she had ever seen. It was as if she had been waiting all her life for this one moment. Their attraction to one another was immediate. He escorted her to the pictures; they shared chocolates and held hands in the back row. Ellie had access to her own private cinema back home, but it did not compare to this.

Besotted and magnetised by one another they went back to his apartment where they made fast and furious love, the like of which Ellie had never experienced. Their clandestine meetings continued for some weeks.

Lanzio, noticing how happy his wife seemed of late, encouraged her to go on meeting with the so-called 'old schoolfriend'. She had even come up with a name, Judith Walker-Symes! In the back of Lanzio's mind the name rang a bell. He'd come across it somewhere before. Ah well, if his wife carried on being happy, that was great, because he was so fed up with this wanting a baby nonsense that he went to have some tests done in secret and was told that he could never become a father.

Suddenly Lanzio remembered where he had heard the name Judith Walker-Symes! Her husband had been an old enemy in the business world, and he recalled reading the obituary column in *The Times* newspaper some time ago of the death of the wife, Judith Walker-Symes, and thinking at the time, rather unkindly, that justice had been meted out.

So, who had his wife really been seeing?

Ellie tore open the oversized brown cardboard envelope. Someone must have sent her an early birthday card. How nice.

Inside, on a stiff piece of card and printed in huge letters with a felt-tip pen were the words "JUDITH WALKER-SYMES IS DEAD". Nothing else. Cold fear washed at Ellie's heart. Was her friend from years ago really dead? She should have looked her up first before using her name as an alibi. She had some quick thinking to do to cover up her tracks. Who could have sent it? Who could have known?

Then she remembered Lanzio always used a thick felt-tip pen when doing his flight plan so that it could be easily read in the air.

But never mind that for now. She had some really good news for Lanzio. She was pregnant at last! He wouldn't have sent her such a message, or would he?

No, of course not. She couldn't wait to see the joy on his face when she would tell him, "You're going to be a father!"

Thoughts on Early Autumn

Combe Martin

3 October 2015

It's that Sunday morning shuttered window feeling as I descend the steep road to the beach.

The early autumn, end of season smells of late cooked breakfasts and half-cooked roast dinners drifting on the air, replacing the ice creams and cream teas of last week.

Wood smoke and coal fires are back, as also are the dogs on the beach having been banned all summer – they rejoice unfettered in and out of the waves with happy raucous barking.

Gone in a weekend the buckets and spades. The surf shop clings on open in the hope of custom. It's wishful thinking. Christmas lunch is advertised in the pub, before the Harvest Festival next week.

It's the season of evening classes, eking out pretend summer, knowing the inevitable winter will come complete with fireworks, flu and Christmas runny noses on school buses and germs in the shops.

Winter fodder repeats itself on TV with boring regularity, programmes all stretched out to make the adverts longer than the actual programme content. I reach for my well-loved books once again.

They never fail to please me as I snuggle down in bed with a hot water bottle.

Ice Cream

South Molton Creative Writing Group
October 2015
True Story

November 30th 1943 and it's my third birthday. Yes, I remember it well, as I recall vividly all my early years in detail; but today I was to have my first ice cream. I had never seen one, let alone tasted one!

The Second World War was in progress and as Mother and I emerged from the air raid shelter we tiptoed over the broken glass and charred wood of the previous night's raid. The acrid smell of burning filled the cold dawn air.

We lived beside a large lake on the outskirts of London, one of our two homes, the other in the West Country. It was easier for Father when home on leave to come home to somewhere central rather than to travel to the far west, that's if we still had a home for him to return to.

Today he was somewhere in the Atlantic.

Mummy wore a red wool costume with reindeer buttons which Daddy sent from Canada. She always looks nice. She has bright red lipstick and Canadian fur boots and gloves. The feather in her hat bounces up and down as she grasps my hand and we set off at too fast a pace for me to barely keep up. I've got a Mickey Mouse gas mask and a dolly bag with my hanky in and a bright new sixpence. We are going to a tube station called Enfield West, but when we get there, there's crowds of people and American soldiers all crammed in the booking hall waiting for a train. Someone says a landmine came in the night and the electric has to be switched on to make the train run. Mummy has a huge crocodile handbag and lets me have a mint lump which she has made. It sticks to my teeth and shuts me up for five minutes, which, she says to someone, is a blessing. I dribble down the velvet collar of my new coat which she made me from an evening gown, along with a horrible peaked hat with elastic which threatens to cut my neck. "Now look what you've done!" and as she bends down to wipe the offending slobber my birthday cards fall out of her bag and onto the floor.

Several American soldiers vie with one another to retrieve them as Mummy is regarded as a 'fashion plate' in red amongst all the sea of grey and khaki clad people.

"Ma'am, is this the birthday girl?" enquires the American.

"Yes, for what it's worth," hisses Mother.

Crouching down, a soldier places his cap on my head, having swiftly removed my horrid elasticated hat.

"You doin' somethin' special, little girl?"

"Yes!" I replied, bursting with pride, "I'm going to have my first ice cream!"

"Say! My little girl has one every day in my country, here's sixpence to buy one from me!"

Mummy says, "No, it's rude to take money from a stranger," and the soldier looks so sad I feel sorry for him.

We get our little green cardboard ticket for the train and the soldiers let us go through first. Sparks flash as the train arrives, the doors swish open. The seat tickles my legs as my feet don't reach the floor. Mummy turns her head away from the "Merrickies," I grin back at them through my fingers. I see my reflection in the train windows as we go underground. I fall asleep and wake up being carried up a moving staircase. We are in London and it's full of damp, smoke, people, clanging bells, and water.

"Where is my ice cream?" I keep asking.

"You'll see," comes Mummy's stock reply.

"I'm tired, I'm hungry." The hand grips tighter. Mummy's going so fast my feet leave the ground. The feather in her hat continues to bounce and her lips go thin. That means I must be quiet, or else.

We enter a huge store called Selfridges. We are in a gold lift with cherubs and flowers on and we go down and get out in something called The Basement. Then we have to go down to another place below the basement, down some steep steps. I'm hanging in air as my arm is on the end of Mummy's hand and my feet don't touch the ground. "Ouch! Where's my ice cream?"

Here's a drab room with pipes going round the walls, and lots of tables and ladies in white caps and aprons and black dresses, called waitresses with little books on a string with a pencil. Everyone looks at Mummy in her red outfit. I feel miserable in my bottle green coat, my feet don't touch the floor when we sit at the table. I get pins and needles.

"Yes?!" demands the black and white waitress.

"Two ice creams please," says Mummy…and "sit up straight for heaven's sake!" I'm tired and can't do as she asks 'cos my feet just won't reach that floor. She rummages in her bag and stands my birthday cards on the table. I feel happy at that, now everyone knows it's my special day. I force myself to keep my eyes open in case I miss the ice cream. Here it comes, on a tray, the black and white waitress is here, when suddenly she swipes all my birthday cards off the table and says, "We don't do that in here!" and plonks the ice cream down. A navy man dressed like Daddy retrieves them and gets Mummy a pot of tea. He sees her special sweetheart navy brooch on her red costume.

The ice cream is in a glass dish on a plate. It is green with a big fan wafer in it and a long spoon. It is too cold and hurts my teeth and face. It tastes like the mint lump I had earlier. I don't really like it.

Suddenly, the lights are flickering, and the plaster is flaking off the walls and the pipes are moving. We are in an air raid and yet everyone is carrying on eating and drinking as if nothing is happening. Muffled thuds rattle the cups on the table. A soldier in khaki serge trousers leans across and protects me, my face feels his rough cloth and I smell his cigarette as he presses my head into him. Somewhere, Vera

Lynn sings *We'll Meet Again*, but the record gets stuck on "sunny day."

"It's a bad 'un up there if we can feel it down here," says the soldier. Mummy just sits there, says nothing, does nothing. Only the soldier puts his arms around me. Perhaps *he* loves me?

Mummy repairs her make-up and another woman eyes her up and down and says she shouldn't be wearing a hat when at the table.

A big wooden bar is lifted off the door and we make our way up the steps to the basement, then to the ground floor. It's cold there, as the whole of the store front is missing. We leave through a maze of corridors to the back of Selfridges.

A landmine had dropped whilst we were in the basement area. The whole of Oxford Street was impassable. So ends my experience of my first ice cream.

FOOTNOTE: I recently looked up the date of my third birthday and a landmine did indeed land overnight just outside Enfield West tube station affecting the line with debris, and a landmine also landed outside Selfridges, and the basement I was in was a Services Personnel room known as the Double Basement, the basement below the basement where food for the Forces and safe shelter could be found.

Dreams and Aspirations

Written for Mental Health Advisory,
Riverside House

The miner dreams at the coal face
Of the day when he can retire
Away from the darkness to 'dayplace'
But for what, to sit by the fire?
To sit by the coal of his labour
And see how it all burns away
To see the black face of his neighbour
Still working and shovelling all day.

Aspiring to walks in the rain
And some fishing, down by the stream
To gaze at the poppies again
But aspiring is only a dream.
As his coughing gobs into spits
And painfully hacks out his soul
Down in the hell of the pits
The nightmare that's stuck in a hole.

The miner dreams of the coal face
Years after the big retire
Away from the darkness to 'dayplace'
In a home that hasn't a fire
To sit by a bowl and a shaver
And see how the nurse turns away
To shave the blank face of his neighbour
Mind gone, but still shovelling all day.

The wheelchair walks in the rain
Where garbage floats on the stream
The nurse breaks the poppies again
The miner goes back to his dream
He coughs in an oxygen mask
And painfully hacks at his soul
"Nurse do me one final task
And get me some water, a bowl."

The miner dreams of the coal face
Of all of the friends he made there
In fact it was not such a bad place
Much better than ending up here.
He places his face in the water
The bubbles rise and then stop
As he slips into the hereafter
Life gone, neck limp, head flop.

An Unfair Judgement

Creative Writing Carers' Group
September 2011
At the time of the Barnstaple Fair

Sabbath, and the austere square Brethren Chapel stood with its door open, ready to devour the congregation with fear, and spit it out afterwards into the forthcoming week.

Ruth demurely followed her parents inside, trembling as she knew what she had coming to her.

As the sermon finished the elders called upon her name.

"Ruth Isaacs, you are to lay prostrate before us and this congregation. You are hereby denounced from this assembly for fraternising with worldly pleasures of the fair last year. You and your unborn child will get you hence never to return. Have you anything to say?"

"Yes. If God is love, then he isn't here!"

The appalled congregation seethed and hissed as, head held high, Ruth marched out, leaving parents, chapel, and black suits behind, clutching the bundle which was thrust at her, the chapel's custom to make sure that a denounced person went away not completely destitute.

But she wasn't with child, she knew that. She was just sick, physically sick of the narrow way of life imposed on her. They had pounced upon her sickness and then tongues were wagging. Thank goodness the fair was returning. It was already setting up along the riverbank. Her heart leapt at the thought of seeing her handsome traveller from last year. Dark haired, strong, oil smeared and sweaty, he was the complete opposite to the lily-livered young chapel men who were being constantly pushed her way.

With hope rising in her heart, she pressed her way forward amongst the throng, bundle hugged tightly to her chest, searching every fairground stall, tent, and ride, even the caravans with their snake-like power cables and washing lines strung up, lights blazing, and the music, colour, and shouting of wares, all assailing her ears and dazzling her eyes. He must be here, her Rory. He said he was returning, and she believed him.

Disconsolately, she sat on the wooden steps of the colourful children's roundabout watching the giant cup-and-saucer, teapot, and milk jug go round containing delighted youngsters. This is where she saw Rory last, where he promised to come back. She had no one else to turn to now and nowhere to go. Surely he must come!

The smell of crushed grass and diesel oil mingled with the fried onions and candyfloss. Curses flew, screams of delight came from pleasure seekers and money changed hands.

The night was pitch black beyond the fringe of ultra-bright lights and still Ruth waited.

Then she saw them, the elders from the chapel. As was their custom they had brought banners to the fair proclaiming *'The End is Near,'* and *'Seek Ye the Lord Whilst He may be Found,'* and *'Repent!'*

One of them was the colporteur that also carried the books and tracts and cycled everywhere to outlying villages.

Such sombre figures in the midst of pleasure. No one was heeding their message until one of the elders spotted Ruth and shouted, "Oh, how the mighty are fallen!" pointing to her.

"Oh ye like sheep have gone astray, look what has happened to this soul beyond redemption, one who refuses to acknowledge wrongdoing, one who is with child and outside the congregation. Woe is you, shame on you!"

Ruth sat transfixed. How could they?

A crowd was gathering. The brethren pointed fingers, the fingers of so-called brotherly love. Tongues lashed like whips, the tongues of the scripture speakers, again and again, for something she hadn't done. The rage of it all spun round and round inside her head, the taunts, shouting and "Leave her alone," spinning like the big wheel; she felt suffocated, trapped, unable to get away as the crowd closed in.

The ride stopped and youngsters climbed out of the teapot and cups and saucers. The proprietor squinted at Ruth over his glasses and beckoned her over.

"You're quite small; quick, get yourself and your bundle into the teapot and we'll start this thing up. They 'religiouses' will soon lose interest if they can't see you to taunt. So long as you don't mind taking on a fellow passenger."

Ruth clambered into the teapot and positioned herself where she could not be seen by the elders. The ride started up and she started to giggle at this ridiculously funny situation. an oversized person in an undersized ride. She kept her head down, trying to stay inconspicuous. The ride came to a halt after a very short time, and someone crammed in beside her, squashing her up. It wasn't a child; it was Rory, grinning from ear to ear, black with oil and grease. As there was no space he 'had' to put his arm around her as they rode round the little track.

"How did you know I was in here?" asked Ruth.

"I was just finishing mending a ride, it was taking ages. Then I was asked to come down here because there were signs of a disturbance. Well the guy who owns this ride said he remembered you, from last year, being with me. He told me

41

what the commotion was about, so here I am. Rory, at your service!"

The ride carried on for longer than normal, until the brethren gave up and moved on, which pleased both the adults hiding in the teapot, and any children lucky enough to have been in a cup-and-saucer.

Later, as Ruth and Rory had supper in his caravan, she told him the story of her demise and he told her she need never worry again as his caravan was now hers as well.

"By the way, what's in the bundle?" Rory asked.

Ruth had not even looked and they both roared with laughter when she opened it and baby clothes came tumbling out.

The Senior Citizens' Christmas Tea

Or 'A Glimmer of Zimmer'
Subject: Write Something about Christmas

Senior citizens in a row
Clutching sticks and glasses
As the tea urn starts to flow
So their water passes.

Out to the loo and back again
"The seat was awful cold!
Had a job to hold it in
I must be getting old!"

Now the choir starts to sing
Lurex ladies warble
On the stage a-bosoming
Double chins a-wobble.

Ancient tinny voices
Up the scale they climb
'Hosanna in excelsis!'
Completely out of time.

Grandpa Glossop, medals on,
Thinks he's in the army
Wants to sing a wartime song
Says everyone is barmy!

Granny's bloomers 'neath her frock
Make a quaint diversion
Vicar reels in genteel shock
Practices aversion!

Now the dentures click as one
Tackling cake and biscuit
One's got stuck in currant bun
No one else will risk it!

Surreptitious goings on
underneath the table
Serviettes and doggy bags
filled as much as able

All too soon it's time to go
into the dark cold night
Happy faces all aglow
a present each, clutched tight

Search

South Molton Creative Writing Group
February 2016

My racing career is over. I've run and done my best. My trainer no longer wants me, and I've given my all for him. I thought he loved me when he said he would search for a new home, but now five of us are trembling in this dark, cold shed as we hear shots in the nearby barn. Our friends we've raced with are killed by the farmer at £10 a time. We've had nothing to eat or drink since our last race. My best race earned my trainer £1,000 and now I am discarded, cold and hungry with only a third of my life spent. When I next see daylight, it will be for the final time, as I am dragged out to the barn.

Voices, rough ones, shouting, then more voices, gentle ones, murmuring. Vans, sliding doors, crates, smell of fear, sudden daylight as the door of the shed opens a crack. Is this it?

"Our search is over," says a female voice. "There are five in here."

The voices are soothing, coaxing, encouraging. We've been rescued from death. I have been bought for £19, not shot for £10. We are led into a van by gentle hands. I guzzle water, devour porridge, and lie on sweet straw. Soft hands stroke me, compassionate eyes look into mine. Blankets cover my shaking body. The Greyhound Rescue people have saved my life, but where am I going?

I feel sick on the sea crossing from Ireland, my land of birth, to a new country, England. Throughout my life my ears have been roughly handled at every race as my green identifications are checked. Not so now; nice hands feel them and stroke my head.

As a puppy, I was bound tight as my ears were forced flat on a wooden block and the green tattoo marks were seared and burnt into my skin.

I finally fall asleep and awake at a rescue centre where I can see dogs of different shapes that I didn't know existed. Our secret language floats around the cages and exercise runs. We've all been rescued, and the search is on to find us new and loving homes.

I am transported hundreds of miles away to a kennels in Devon, but no one wants me 'cos I'm black. I'm fed and walked, and they are kind, but I'm getting nervous as I worry too much. After six months I go to a foster home. This is nice, it's warm and cosy but I am afraid and don't trust anyone. They don't like me because I don't join in, I shake most of the time.

"We wanted a friendly dog," they said, so off I go to another place which I hated as children poked and screamed at me when the adults weren't looking.

"This dog is vicious with children!" they lied. "Take it away."

So they lost my vaccination papers and I got shunted to another kennels in Cornwall, a step backwards perhaps, to ending up somewhere worse.

The boring kennel routine was interrupted one day by the sound of a van and more sliding doors. There was a good scent on the air. I was given a quick brush down and led into the office area where I was let off. I ran straight over to a lady sitting with her arms outstretched and felt her wave of love for me, and as she stroked me our eyes met, and I saw a tear in hers. I knew then that my search for a loving owner was over. An instant bond had been struck between us.

Later, in the van, I curled up into a tight little ball on a comfy bed as we sped towards my new forever home.

The Homecoming

Creative Writing Carers' Group
Write about a Christmas card received

A stretched blue canvas sky
Backdrops storm-tinged cloud
A ship comes sailing by
So tall and mighty proud.

Vessels all around her
Make way as she glides past
With five majestic sails
For every flag-topped mast.

A tight and choppy sea
Warns of a storm ahead
And smoke stacks in the lee
Have already fled.

Distant harbour beckons
Light dances on the bay
And every skipper reckons
to be home by end of day.

Salt encrusted faces
Look towards the land
Home from foreign places
Oh! The feeling's grand

Rowers, barges, tugs,
And on the harbour wall
Embraces, kisses, hugs,
Will come to most, not all –

The seven seas

Make widow's weeds.

A Labour of Love

Creative Writing Carers' Group
February 2012
Subject: Snow

The lights of the house shone out in the distance and the stars twinkled on the frost as the heavily pregnant mum tried to negotiate the path to home. She was too weak and weary to go on; even her friends decided to rest.

She went into labour late in the freezing night and when dawn came she could not see properly… no trees, no sky, no house – just blankness and a few shadowy bodies in the muffled half-light. Gasping for air, she shifted around but could not get comfortable because everything was pressing in on her head, on her body. It was different when she had had the twins. How she remembered that day, cocooned in warmth and being waited on!

She called out but her companions, the shadowy ones, did not reply – they were dead. So she was alone and as the birth pains increased, so did her thirst. Oh for some water, some warmth, and the company of others! A faint trickle of moisture dribbled down the wall of her 'tomb', and with her tongue she licked at it like a dog. So it had come to this! Never had she imagined, during the long hot summer days of plenty, that she would end up like this when her time came to give birth. She was getting colder and needed another coat, as the one she was wearing was now laden with frost and icicles. Pain shot through her body as she tried to give birth again, and with the new day the shadowy 'tomb' turned a blue-grey colour – just a bit brighter – and with it, fresh fear and terror as the place shook and vibrated with thudding, muffled at first but getting ever nearer and louder.

Thud! Thud! THUD!

At the loudest and most frightening moment of all, she gave birth and saw a precious new life arrive, just as hers faded away.

Slowly and tenderly the shepherd lifted the new born lamb out of the snow drift.

Summer

Creative Writing Carers' Group
July 2012
Subject: Summer

The darkness is filled with a hush of expectancy across the vast landscape. There is stillness and silence, apart from a few whispers and movements in that moment before dawn.

Dewy grass is fragrant where bodies have crushed it whilst turning over in a fitful doze.

This is it; the time is almost here.

The people rise up to greet that imperceptible moment when the light of a new day comes, just before sun up.

The mammoth stones, that were black and forbidding, are now a brilliant cathedral, a picture frame filled with the golden sun. Stonehenge.

The faithful from all walks of life now raise their hands and faces to greet the summer solstice. It was worth the long night time vigil!

Whispers now become voices, happy, jubilant, each praising their individual god. Fashion, class, creed, all become one in this shared experience.

A tambourine jingles gently, a lone flute sings to the henge, its liquid note soaring upwards with the first skylark of the day. A steady drum beat mirrors the people's own heartbeat and their rejoicing, especially for one happy couple.

As the girl turns to the man she can see the dawn light reflected in his loving eyes.

He tenderly holds her hand and asks, "Have you come to a decision yet, for the naming ceremony of our darling daughter later today?"

"Oh yes," she replies, "a name to capture this moment for ever. Her name shall be Summer."

The Wave

Creative Writing Prompt
Write something positive about a picture that
we were given.

For several days now, the anchorage in the inlet had been deserted. The weather for early June had been cold with high seas and, despite the full moon at night, it had been dark. Where had all the little boats gone?

Dorothy had spent those days and nights wondering ever since her father and her sweetheart David had silently disappeared with grim faces, wearing old clothes, and carrying hastily-packed sandwiches. Father barely embraced Mother and David only gave Dorothy a peck on the cheek.

Then they slipped their mooring in silence into the darkness of the night.

Other boats' wakes could be glimpsed in flashes; the overall quietness hung heavy as a shroud, as boat after boat on the water disappeared.

Dorothy used David's bicycle to get to the waterfront each day to await his return. Sitting on the bench in the glorious sunshine she could not imagine life without him.

The cruelty of war clawed at her heart like a vicious cat. She was in love with David! So sudden was this revelation that tears stung her eyes to think that she might never see him again. She fondly touched his bicycle, recalling the primroses he had picked for her as they strolled along a country lane... simple pleasures that had meant so much.

Her tear drops rolled down onto the bicycle frame, as she hugged the big old saddlebag that smelled of leather, and she wept her heart out. The beautiful day of glorious light and sparkling water meant nothing to her. How could he go off to war? He wasn't even a soldier; he was gentle and kind and loved mending the boats on the river.

With her head bowed, and the sun getting higher, she sat there absorbed in her misery, looking at the ground. Her heart ached for David. She wished she could have told him how much he meant to her, so that he could carry it with him to the place that only he knew about.

As the afternoon shadows lengthened, Dorothy raised her head to see a small flotilla of boats appear in the inlet. Surely these were not the same ones that went out? They were, but, in silence they returned with a heavy air about them: bullet-ridden, broken-masted, and the men in them bloodstained and aged beyond their years. Their eyes had seen carnage as they had gone to rescue the troops stranded on the coast of France.

Their job done, they were home, but not all of them. Dorothy strained her tear-stained eyes to seek out David. She waited, then, around the wooded headland the boat appeared, but oh, so slowly! Then she saw him, and she was willing the vessel to go faster. Could he see her?

Dorothy took off her blouse in happy abandonment and waved it with both hands so that he could see her. It seemed to take an age before the gap between the boat and land would close, and forever to tie up alongside. He had seen her alright, but he had two whole days and nights of bloody history and carnage locked up in his head – he might tell her one day.

But for now, in silence, he went to her on the quayside. She saw his pain and weariness, he saw her freshness and sweetness, and as he savoured the English air, he buried his head in her hair and whispered, "You smell of summertime, and I love you."

Past and Future

I'm riding high on my father's shoulders. He is in his naval officer's uniform. I am in a 'war zone' on Braunton Burrows amongst rows of tents, Jeeps, and cookhouse smells. From my lofty height I look down on many American soldiers, and they smile back at me and wave.

The Second World War is in progress and these are the 'practice for killing' grounds. Sand is whipped up by the wind, the environment unfriendly, as grit and dirt churned up by passing Jeeps grinds into teeth and eyes.

My father's escort carries his document case. We meet an important American general and enter a large tent. A coffee aroma fills the place, and I am given chocolate and chewing gum from a culture far removed from my own. I am also given a biro pen; what fun as I've never seen one before! I start drawing what I see.

There are charts and maps on an improvised board, a long stick for pointing, card tables with papers and books, strange khaki-coloured radios and receivers. Father sits at one of these with his earphones on. The Americans are in deep conversation. Father decodes the Morse signals as I draw.

I am in heaven, as a fizzy drink is given to me. These kind Americans far from their homeland have a self-contained community radiating friendliness to a little girl who, no doubt, reminds them of their own families.

The late afternoon draws on into evening. The talking has ended. The general lights up a huge cigar. Father is offered one but cannot cope with it: it's too big!

It's getting cold, but the general wraps his warm arms around me and puts me into his Jeep in one easy movement, cigar still in his mouth. I cough with the smoke of it and complain that I cannot see. He says to Father and me that we will soon 'see' something that we will remember in years to come.

The general is smiling to himself as we reach a vantage point and stop. His eyes crease at the corners as he points to a house in the distance on the cliff top. The setting sun is playing red fire on the windows. Is this what he means, I wonder? Father nods his head and tells the general, "Your secret is safe with me."

"What secret?" I ask.

"Never you mind," was the standard adult reply.

The war ended; the Americans departed. Reminders of their existence surfaced from time to time. The American road that they had built, rusty iron slabs refusing to die, old barbed wire, rotting sand bags.

I grew up wandering and exploring the burrows area, painting and photographing its wildlife, the dragonflies in the slacks, the exquisite sand pansies, the orchids. My first solo exhibition included the dykes and stiles, swans, and boats, all painted on location at the burrows.

Then one day, there was a sale of art materials at a place called Preston House at Saunton. This was on the cliff top overlooking the whole of the burrows. This was the house that the American general had pointed out all those years ago.

My excitement mounted as I entered it, beholding the most lovely plasterwork on the stairway wall and ceiling. A calm, solid house, dim filtered light from a stained-glass window creating a sense of peace.

I realised that I knew the owners and was shown around, and they let me into their secret – yes; and I hung onto every word.

They told me that the Prime Minister, Winston Churchill, stayed in this very house during World War Two to be close to certain manoeuvres concerning the Americans. It also gave Winston, an accomplished artist, a rare chance to paint the astonishing view from the window unobserved. I kept my counsel and said nothing.

I moved out of the area to West Somerset and into the future, sixty-five years down the line from my visit to the American camp.

A newspaper article grabbed my attention! Preston House was going to be demolished to make way for holiday flats and someone had written that Preston House was an important piece of local history for Braunton, not just because of its unique plasterwork but because there was a rumour that Prime Minister Winston Churchill had stayed there during a crucial stage in World War Two: and did anyone know about this? Could this building be preserved if it played such an important but secret part in the war? Was it even true?

I replied to the article with my story, but sadly nothing was done, and when I next visited the area I walked past Preston House, sunk in on itself, dying in its overgrown garden.

In a last desperate visit to Braunton Museum with my story, I was met with disinterest.

But times move on. A new culture sprung up to embrace the whole Burrows area, making it a conservation place, nurturing wildlife. Visitors came and left with a sense of wellbeing, helping in turn the local economy and this new area which became known as the North Devon Biosphere.

The sands of time have all but erased the tank tracks of war and, as the sea nibbles at the edges of the dunes, I am aware that in my now later years I am a piece of living history and soon my memories will be lost forever, of the evening when the American general pointed to Preston House with its windows red in the setting sun, containing its special secret.

But then, perhaps, these written memories might come to someone's attention and be saved for all time in an archive for future historians to enjoy.

Oh yes! I was there, chocolate, chewing gum, biro, and all!

I Decided to Enter This World

South Molton Writing Group
Subject was the first line from a book:
"I decided to enter this world"

I decided to enter this world as a dog, with a human brain. It was my choice. I could have come back as a human with a dog's brain.

Having been a human last time around, I had observed my dog and other dogs and how they tried to communicate with me; so, with this in mind, I thought I could have a very interesting, if bit shorter life. So I said 'Yes' to the Great I Am and with that, he placed me on my journey.

I emerged warm, pushed, and shoved and licked all over thinking like a human but squeaking like a pup. I couldn't see anything at first but could understand the humans' 'oohs' and 'ahs'. It was a bit degrading having to suck nipples instead of drinking a good old cuppa tea. Puppy food wasn't much better either, it was all mushy, but worse was to come. That dog food from cans really does stink and stays around one's whiskers all day. There were nine of us puppies with our feet in the trough until there was no more room as we had grown apace.

The humans were discussing how much we were worth

and where to sell us. I was dreading leaving this home as the lady was especially kind to me and called me her favourite. I fixed my eyes on her and spoke to her in my head, turning it this way and that, I looked longingly at her.

"I'm definitely special," I gazed. "Can I stay here?"

"Oh look!" she exclaimed to her husband. "That dog is almost human, see how it practically talks to us?"

One by one, my brothers and sisters were taken away to new homes and it was just me left. It was now or never! I started picking up things around the house and putting them back where they belonged. I fetched the post; I knew when the humans were going shopping and I fetched the bag. They said they were leaving at nine o'clock and I stood and barked nine times looking at said clock.

"That dog even knows the time, I'm sure of it," said the lady of the house.

"It's just coincidence," replied the man.

One morning it was getting late and they had almost overslept, so I mischievously crept into their bedroom and did the loudest bark possible right in the man's ear. "What the bucking broncos did you do that for?" the man shouted. Then he saw what time it was and without any modesty, careered off to the bathroom naked. That was a laugh! I was hastily chucked some breakfast as the man went off to work.

I carried the newspaper from the letterbox to the lady of the house. She patted my head and after a quick read she spread some onto the floor and put my water bowl on it. Of course, I stood there reading it and tried to turn the page over to see if page three still had naughty ladies on it.

"I swear that dog can read!" said the lady of the house later, when the man had returned home. "Rubbish!" he said, "You've got a vivid imagination, that's all." With that, I threw the lead at him and demanded a walk.

Some months later, that lovely lady of the house received some bad news and she bade me sit by her and listen as she cried her eyes out and sobbed into my coat. A discarded letter lay on the floor. I read the report from the hospital. She only had a short time left. I already knew that something was wrong. I cuddled up to her as much as possible in the days to come and carried things for her, picked up that which she dropped and finished off food that she could not eat. I stayed by her bed and loved her as much as I could. "That dog gets more of a look-in than I do," said the man. Soon, many medics and nurses were coming and going, and the man stopped going to work. I steadfastly stayed by the bed where the lady of the house could put her hand down to touch my head. The carers wanted me out, but I refused, and then came the day when no hand came down to touch me and I could smell a change and my darling lady whispered goodbye to me and said I was better than any human she had ever known. I swallowed a big lump in my throat and cried.

For some weeks afterwards, I was only given short walks and left on my own all day. I had a look through the TV paper and relieved my boredom by pressing the remote buttons but never getting the right channels as my paws were too big. The man used to swear he had turned the TV off but found it on, when he returned home, by which time I was supposedly snoozing in my bed but with one eye open. I tried to comfort him in the evenings, but he kept pushing me away. He took to drinking at night and drowning his sorrow and forgetting to let me out no matter how much I asked and in the end I couldn't hold it in. He got very angry with me and I hid under the table. He crashed into it, I ran out, and the teapot fell on my back and the pain of boiling hot liquid made me scream and scream. The neighbours came running. "Just put me out of my agony!" I howled. I couldn't stop. Someone put a cold wet towel on me. The man couldn't drive me to the vet because he'd had too much booze in his system from the night before.

"The vet will have to come here," one of the neighbours suggested. "This poor dog is in no state to be moved."

Oh, the pain! How I wished that dear lady of the house was still here to comfort me; she always understood.

The man stood on the side-lines gibbering. The vet and his assistant nurse arrived. The neighbours looked on. I felt as if on fire. I pleaded and pleaded with my eyes to the vet to help me, I even thumped my tail slightly. The room seemed to be coming and going, the faces were worried and white. The vet said it was time for me to go and asked the man's permission to put me to sleep.

The man was distraught as he realised the error of his recent ways. He said he was sorry and so sad. He held my head and I wished the vet would hurry up and end my distress.

"Do you forgive me?" sobbed the man. "I'm so ashamed of myself."

Six Days On and One Day Off

South Molton Creative Writing Group
November 2014
This is a true story about Lundy in winter
Subject: The group each placed random items on the
table which were to be included in the story. The
items were: dice, computer mouse, mushroom, two
grapes, Lundy keys, a cooking apple, a heart
(*presumably not a real one*), pony plaque.

"In an emergency, the life raft is under your seat. Whatever you do, remember, pull out the stopper to inflate it AFTER you leave the helicopter or none of us will get out!"

As I was co-pilot, I had heard it all before as we made the short flight back from Hartland Point to Lundy Island, a matter of twelve minutes.

I was returning after a weekend break on the mainland; it was either one month on the island and a weekend off, or three months on the island with one week off.

In January and February there were no holiday makers or writers, and this was the time of deep-cleaning, painting, and mending properties. Also there was the ongoing 'rhodo' bashing and rat baiting stations, path, wall, and road maintenance. The island's supply vessel, the Oldenburg, stopped sailing in the winter.

As we approached the island the jokey pilot announced, "Touchdown inevitable! Crash or otherwise!"

From the air, the seemingly tiny church of Saint Helena now rapidly came up to meet us, revealing its full size, and we disgorged onto the rough field, rotor blades still turning, whilst a tractor and trailer was being quickly loaded with supplies.

Pulling my hood up against the cold easterly wind, I squelched my way to the Tavern, the Island's main hub, eating, and meeting place. Bursting into the Tavern, bringing the cold air with me, fellow workers looked up, muttering friendly curses about letting in the freeze up. They picked up their bags to make their way out to the helicopter and home to the mainland – their work stint finished and mine just beginning. Strewn across the table were the remnants of their half-finished games with dice, chess, and cards hastily discarded.

The familiar rude greetings from the rest of the staff followed me up the wooden stairs to the island's office and nerve centre. The computer screen lay dormant, complete with its sleeping mouse, and I picked up my Lundy keys from the pigeon-hole and saw, yet again, that I had been consigned to the staff caravan, a rickety construction tucked down low under a wall away from the prevailing wind and tethered to rocks with metal cables. With the easterly wind now howling into a gale, I hung onto the walls along the track and reached my 'tin box'. I could barely hang on to the caravan door as it smacked back onto the side. The whole thing was rocking, and the big canister of water on the table shifted around like a tidal wave. It was impossible to light the gas stove as the wind crept in all the gaps and blew the match out.

As I had been awake for eighteen hours and I wasn't due to start any work until the morrow, I lay on the bunk exhausted and being tossed around as if at sea, such was the severity of the weather.

At daybreak, the sound of hail stones on the metal roof awoke me and it was bitterly cold. Looking towards the mainland I could see pink snow on Exmoor touched by the rising sun.

I made my way to the Tavern as other staff members drifted in. At 8am we sat around a huge table with an industrial toaster as the centrepiece plus a big urn of tea. The week's rota was handed out and I studied mine. I would be responsible for feeding the ponies, collecting chicken eggs, and finishing off some stone walling. Also cleaning the church, plus any job in between.

As the toaster stopped spewing out char-grilled masterpieces, we drained our mugs of tea and went our separate ways.

I leaned into the wind, my overtrousers flapping and, donning my industrial gloves, I hitched the trailer to the quad-bike and loaded up some pony nuts and fodder, under the rattling corrugated roof of the store.

Bouncing along the 'M1', the nickname for the rough track which goes centrally down the length of the island, I turned off by the quarter wall to where I knew the ponies would be sheltering. It was even rougher going over the wild tussocky landscape and I was reminded that my correct sitting position must be mastered, or I would be thrown off! Duty done, ponies fed, I returned to base and the welcome of the Tavern fire.

I finished my stonewalling section the next day and joined the shepherd in the lambing shed where the first new-born lambs were steaming wet on the straw. Radio One was playing day and night to keep all the expectant mums company and a generator was rigged up for light there at night as all power on the island goes off at midnight until 6am.

My working week passed quickly and, hoping for a settled break in the weather, I looked forward to Sunday, my day off. The morning dawned bright and clear but with a south-westerly shift. I was restless to get going! After checking the island weather report and with due regard to wind and tide I contacted the island warden and let him know where I was going and the approximate time of my return. This was one of the few windows of opportunity in the year where the tide would be low enough for me to attempt a longstanding ambition, to get into a certain cave that went from one side of Rat Island and emerged out onto the opposite side.

Hoisting my backpack and rather heavy filming equipment, I happily strode down the 400-foot descent from the top of the island to the landing bay, on the way passing through the ruins of the ancient kitchen gardens of Millcombe House, which amazingly still held the remnants of two withered grapes clinging to the walls in this sheltered valley. I had once picked a huge parasol mushroom from here, providing me with a delicious fry-up.

When I got to the landing bay I had to reach my objective. To do this, I had to negotiate a tricky section called the Devil's Kitchen, a slow laborious scramble around slippery rocks and razor-sharp barnacles. There was no time to hang about as the tide would be turning to come in again within the hour and I needed every precious minute if I was to make a dramatic film inside the long tunnel-like cave.

Feeling excited yet frightened, I came to the entrance and removed my boots and hung them by the laces around my neck as the bottom of the cave was partially flooded. From brilliant sunlight, I stepped into a damp and echoing gloom, the cave walls mocking me with their eerie sound as my feet froze with shock in the cold water. The wind came from nowhere and whistled through the tunnel. I could just see light at the other end but I had a long way to go, and the further I went, the narrower and lower the cave became.

I decided to turn back about halfway. I really didn't like the spooky atmosphere and the claustrophobic feeling, but I had filmed some very good sequences. Never mind that I didn't reach the other end.

Anxiety began to set in and almost turned to panic. Supposing something happened in here?

And then it did! I stubbed my foot on a submerged rock and fell headlong, my backpack propelling me forward with its momentum, my camera clattering along the cave floor and my recently operated-on knee took the full impact. Fright, shock, and a desperate sense of urgency to get out of that place got me going.

Then I saw red! It belonged to me! It was my blood flowing from cut hands and oozing through my trousers from my knee. What damage had I done?

Amazingly my boots were still tied around my neck, soaking wet of course. I got into a deep rock pool, keeping my clothes on to keep warm, and soaked my injuries in the salt water. With chattering teeth I rescued my first aid kit and flask of tea from my backpack and chewed some energy bars. I patched up my hands, and shakily stood up. Checking my camera I discovered, to my horror, that the battery was missing! It must have dropped out when I fell over!

I just had to go back in there and find it. Yes, like a needle in a haystack, even though the battery was the size of a matchbox, so expensive it would take ages to save up for another one. I was absolutely terrified. Could I go back in there after all that had happened? Was there time before the tide started to turn? As I re-entered the cave, I thought, 'well, I have done some dangerous things in my time,' but this was the ultimate challenge. It took nerve but, when I reached the spot where I fell, I miraculously found the battery and it worked.

A subtle change was in the air of the cave, a different smell and a strengthening vacuum of the wind passing through. The tide *was* on the turn. Now I had a race against time. I had to caution myself not to rush and fall again as I would never get out alive.

Reaching the cave exit, I saw the mighty breakers heaving and crashing on the rocks. With luck and determination, and a pounding heart, I broke the pain barrier and scrambled through the Devil's Kitchen, panting and blowing for all I was worth. As the water kept grabbing at my back I felt the Devil himself was trying to get me.

Then an amazing thing happened. I felt my hands and feet being placed in the familiar crevices and hand holds of the Devil's Kitchen. I was safe! I didn't do it, but some force for the good had saved me! I promised all sorts of things I would do better in my life in that instant.

Later, upon reviewing my film, I saw a giant golden hand lifting me out of the Devil's Kitchen, just that once, for I never saw it again, no matter how many times I re-ran it.

FOOT NOTE:

When the warden asked me if I had managed to do my filming I said, "Yes."

He said, "You were lucky: a big swell out in the Atlantic had made the tide come in half an hour early."

Flowers in the Cradle

South Molton Group
March 2015
Occupations were put in a hat; I pulled out
CARPENTER

Will put the finishing touches to the cradle that would be home to his firstborn. He had to admit that it was a beautiful object, made with such love for the woman he loved. Only yesterday, he was finishing and smoothing down a coffin, such was the diversity of his carpentry skills in this tiny remote community, which earned a precarious living on the wind lashed shores of this fishing outpost.

Tomorrow, at first light, he would be sailing on the tide, as all hands were needed regardless of occupation, to race to the fishing grounds to harvest the migrating fish far out to the west, food to salt down and see the community through the harsh winter.

Bethany was lighting the oil lamps and putting the gruel to soak overnight on the banked down peat fire. Why did Will have to go now, just as she was so near her time? She wished he could be here, but everyone helped everyone else when a community effort was needed.

Will watched as his young wife lovingly tended to domesticity in the lamplight. She tucked a stray strand of long hair behind her ear and gave him a smile. His weather worn face was full of love as he produced the cradle he had made with his roughened hands, those hands that could be so gentle as Bethany well knew.

She looked with pleasure at the beautiful cradle and pictured the baby that would soon be in it, as did Will.

Knowing that their remaining time together was short, they shared their meal in the flickering lamplight, eyes shining at each other and repaired to bed early, content just to lie in each other's embrace.

A brassy dawn was breaking over a sullen sea as the whole community collected on the quay side to witness the departure of the two fishing boats. The water seethed and gnashed at the skirts of seaweed fringing the sea wall.

Will hoisted his leather bag of tools onto his shoulder, the carpentry tools that his father had passed on to him. He knew each tool as an intimate friend, for his hand fitted their shapes like no other. The other bag contained hard bread and tack, laver cakes and dried fish for the journey.

As he went off with the tide, he could see Bethany outlined against the rising sun, her long skirt and hair blowing in the breeze, her swollen body beautiful in his eyes. Her tears flowed into the sea until she could see him no more. The two boats had finally disappeared over the wall of the world.

The further the fishing boats travelled, the nearer Bethany's time grew, until, it seemed, poised on an unfathomable abyss, her baby entered the world with a wild cry, just as Will's cry was whipped away on the wind of a storm as his boat sank.

Each day, Bethany waited with others for the joyous return of the pair of fishing boats, willing for them to come. Her fine baby son, her joy, she longed to share with Will.

The weather cleared and a shout went up from the spotter on High Rock. A boat in sight! Bethany detached the baby from her breast and drew her shawl close. The distant smudge appeared back over the wall of the world, but oh so slowly!

The excited gathering that fell silent. One lone and battered vessel with a cargo of dejection. Grim faces, no catch, no voices, no rejoicing. Ropes thrown and caught in the age-old fashion, hitched and tied. Silence. Huge silence. So heavy. The aura of doom hung all about. Just the sound of water nibbling at the edges. Even the gulls were absent.

It was not Will's boat. Silence, then as news broke of his boat sunk with all hands, the waiting began. The storm had taken the boat with a full catch of fish. The other boat with only half a catch had survived and had stayed as long as they had dared to look for survivors, but their view was blotted.

Bethany and the other womenfolk consoled each other in their tide of sorrow. It was definite, all hands lost. They had many mouths to feed and no work. But Bethany only had one mouth to feed and as the months went by she took it upon herself to look after all the little ones as women worked at their looms and knitting: true cottage industry. The pieces were taken by pack horse overland and sold in the far-off towns.

As the months rolled into seasons, and seasons into years, it was agreed that a simple wooden memorial be placed in the little burial ground on the hill with the names of the lost souls to be carved upon it. And so it was placed inside the circle of white stones, five long years after the tragedy. The whole community made the climb into the mist-shrouded hill and remembered.

Then began the repair from despair. Some of the women re-married and had babies. Out of death had come new life.

Will knew it was coming, he sensed it in his bones that fateful morning when he left Bethany standing on the quay, with the brassy sky and sullen sea all around. He knew he shouldn't have gone, but times were hard, and he needed the extra work. As the storm approached he had tied his tool bag to his body. They said he was mad; he'd drown quicker than all of them put together. He felt calmer with his father's old tools close to him, if he was going to his death then he was comforted in a small way.

As the boat's planks and timbers came apart, he lashed himself to one of these in a last desperate hope of survival. It was everyman for himself as abandon ship was declared.

The roaring and screaming was still in his head when he was dumped by the merciless sea onto a beach, far from habitation as far as he could painfully see. No smoke, no sheep, nothing except for the fishing boat's smashed up timbers and lockers strewn along the strandline. Great welts had gouged his flesh from where the ropes had lashed him to the plank. His sodden tool bag had also survived.

He caught fish and crab with the tangled lines from the wreck. He gathered dried sphagnum moss for tinder and waited for the sun to heat the broken glass he'd found, to set light to it, piling driftwood round it to make a fire. He built himself a shelter from the ship's timbers and he foraged on the sparse wind-blown landscape.

He was sad as he thought of the baby he would in all likelihood never see, and poor Bethany. His body ached as he recalled their final evening together and how lovely she had looked in the lamplight. Tonight, he would build a big fire before setting off inland to seek out civilization if there was any.

The shepherd gazed out of his hovel on the top of the slight rise and saw the fire reflected in the night sky. It was the wrong time of the year for the Northern Lights. It was far off, in the land of no trees and no people. Tomorrow, he would look when he had driven his sheep to the beach to feed on the vitamin-enriched seaweed.

Will spotted sheep on the rocks; there must be a shepherd somewhere! His hopes were not long in being raised as the old bearded man appeared. He looked astonished to see Will, for Will was running to him, but neither could understand each other for their languages were different.

They befriended one another and Will spent the next few years helping the old man and dwelling with his people until a pack horse and rider, that had strayed off route in the fog, appeared in the wilderness.

The rider understood Will's dialect and Will recognised the weaving pattern of his own community in the cloth that he was shown.

And so began his farewell to the kind people, as he began his long journey criss-crossing the landscape towards his homeplace, following as directed the white stones placed on the high inland moorland routes, those white guides that stood out in the sudden swirls of fog. One step either side could mean death in a bog.

A radiant sunrise bathed the community in splendour. Will saw his name etched on the memorial atop the little hill surrounded by white stones.

One by one, the people down below shook off sleep and started about their daily chores. Will remained hidden behind a stone and squinted in the early morning light down towards his old turf-roofed dwelling. It had grown in his long absence. The peat fire's acrid tang smelled as fragrant as roses to William. Oh Bethany was going to have a surprise. That is, if she was still alive!

And then he saw her, with a young boy hanging on to her long skirt, his son! He wanted to run straight down to them and shout out his arrival! But no, he waited, and his spirits sank as he saw other children emerge from the dwelling. She must have presumed him dead, and re-married, certainly the memorial suggested it as all the other crew members' names from his boat were inscribed upon it.

He didn't want to upset her new life, but he had nowhere else to go. He looked gaunt and had aged. If she didn't want him, then at least he had a son and he owed it to the boy to be his father.

The shout went up from the lookout on High Rock that there was a stranger in the camp.

Everyone came out to look at this thin bearded man in tattered clothing picking his way down the hillside. Who could it be? Not many travellers passed this way.

Bethany knew who it was, for Will still had the old tool bag strung across his person. She wanted to run to him but stood rooted to the spot. The children sensed the atmosphere and clung to her.

As he drew near, she saw the tears streaking the dust on his face and beard. He took off his bag and looked questionably at the children gathered around Bethany and asked her if she had handfasted in marriage in his absence. If so, he would leave her in peace. He waited for her answer, his whole world stood still for an eternity as he remembered all the hope, hardship, and pain that he had gone through to reach this moment.

This moment, this longing, his people, his home, his child, his Bethany.

One by one the people came and took the children from Bethany, all except the one child, and he knew without a doubt that this was his son.

Bethany raised her hand to his and said for all to hear that she had not handfasted in marriage in his absence, her hand was still his and that all the children belonged to others in the community.

There was great rejoicing that day with feasting and happiness for the couple and their little boy.

Each community member brought them a gift, be it a stone, a flower, a sweetmeat, or a turf for the fire.

Later that night, Will stood beside the cradle that he had made with such love. A pot of wild herbs rested in it. Bethany had placed them there. Will tenderly picked them up and gave them to Bethany. No longer would she have to put flowers in the cradle for, hopefully, soon they would be replacing them with another love child.

The Spirit of Hope

Ilfracombe Writers' Group
January 2019
Subject: Hope

It was hot outside, even at this early hour of 10:30am, the time that the exhibition was supposed to open. After walking around for ages and re-acquainting myself with Dulverton, I returned to find that the exhibition was still shut. Had I made this sentimental journey for nothing? I enquired at the adjoining library.

"Oh, the caretaker hasn't opened up. Come back in half an hour," they said, and I did.

The cool interior of the heritage centre matched the coolness of the two stewards on duty.

I was the first visitor in there and my shoes squeaked on the newly polished floor, disturbing the hush that one used to get in a library.

"Ahem! I say!"

I felt eyes boring into my back.

"A donation if you please, and it's that way round and keep inside the rope!"

I looked at the two stewards. Frosty Face and Baldy Blazer.

"It says it's free on the information board outside," I replied.

A worn-out video started playing by the tired book display, destroying what was left of a pleasant atmosphere. I stood my ground, blocking it out and stared in fascination and wonder at the exhibits imprisoned inside glass cabinets. Some of the items I had actually handled in the past, on Exmoor.

This is what I had come all this way to see. There was a haversack and groundsheet, memories of a shared impromptu picnic at Mole's Chamber, a faded scarf nearly lost in the sudden gust of wind high up on Sandy Way, the wellies still caked in moorland mud, the lambing knife, now the sketches, paintings and all of a fellow artist's paraphernalia, the watercolour paints, pans, palettes, and oh so many brushes standing sentry in the old tall containers. What images were conveyed down those handles and with what care they had been cleaned and reshaped to a point after each use.

The paper too, from posh, thick Bockingford to down-and-out bits of old sketch pads, the water pots, half-finished drawings with notes. The Spirit of Hope Bourne trapped behind glass? No! That was not her way. She would want to be out of there, striding on the high moor where my husband and I had the privilege of painting and sharing materials with her. Such memories!

Lining my camera up to record this one final precious reminder of the display in the glass cabinet I felt somehow I would release her into the elements where she belonged when,

"You can't do that in here! Photographs are forbidden!"

I was so wrapped up with the happy times the three of us spent together, and how Hope fulfilled her promise of attending my solo exhibition, that I had almost forgotten Frosty Face and Baldy Blazer.

"You buy the video instead, and the books!"

Well, I had already got the books, some signed by the good lady herself. I decided to exit the exhibition and as I foot squeaked behind a display stand with my camera and backpack I overheard Frosty Face remark to Baldy Blazer, "Hmph! Typical visitor! All they want is to take a photo to say, 'Been there, done that.' What do they know about Hope Bourne?"

I returned and, facing them, said, "Alizarin Crimson, Ultramarine, and a little Light Red. That is what I know about Hope; her favourite combination of colours for a pale mauvey wash to create the distance of an Exmoor horizon meeting heather and sky; her words, her description. Been there, done that, *with her.*"

Frosty Face and Baldy Blazer went a little Light Red!

About the Author

Anne Beer

Anne Beer has lived a life so full you wonder where to begin. She has endured great hardship and sorrow as well as enjoying many happy times too. Since she is writing her memoirs I will save the best for then, but if you have read this book already then you will know she was a qualified helicopter pilot and that's just a small part of her talents.

Anne began writing at an age when most children are just beginning to read for themselves and she has a natural gift for painting and drawing, a gift which she has nurtured alongside such greats as Hope Bourne.

Anne now lives in North Devon with her beautiful and placid assistance dog Ellie. This book is, I hope, the first of several, since there are many more stories just as good still to be typed up in addition to the above-mentioned memoir which, if and when it is finished, will be one of the most interesting books ever to be published.

Blue Poppy Publishing

To reiterate what was said at the start of this book, we would love to see online reviews, but we would also particularly love to get actual physical handwritten letters, because Anne does not own a computer, laptop, tablet, or smartphone.

You can write to her at:

Anne Beer,
c/o Blue Poppy Publishing,
2 Oxford Grove,
Ilfracombe,
Devon,
EX34 9H

It would mean an awful lot to her.

ALSO AVAILABLE:

We offer a range of books, mostly by local authors from Devon. These include picture books for young children, chapter books for older children, YA novels, historical fiction, thrillers, memoirs, and non-fiction including a wonderful cookery book with strong Devon connections.

You can order all our books in any good bookshop or direct from our website www.bluepoppypublishing.co.uk